W9-CIR-549

UNCLE·LUBIN

THE ADVENTURES OF UNCLE LUBIN

TOLD AND ILLUSTRATED
BY
W. HEATH ROBINSON

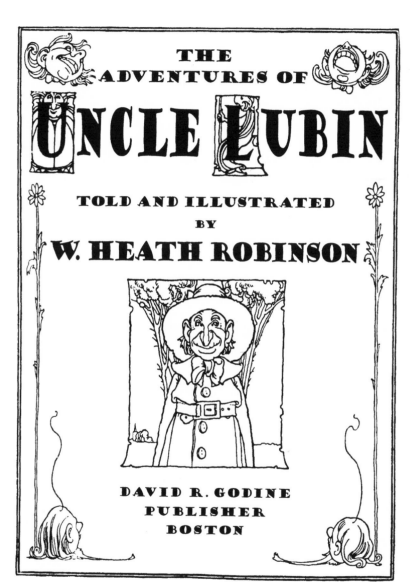

DAVID R. GODINE
PUBLISHER
BOSTON

This edition is dedicated to the Williamson family, whose fondness for
Uncle Lubin has lasted through four generations, and whose dog-eared first edition
allowed the present one to see the light of day.

Published in 1992 by
David R. Godine, Publisher, Inc.,
Post Office Box 450
Jaffrey, New Hampshire 03452
www.godine.com

All rights reserved. No part of this book may be used or reproduced in any
manner whatsoever without written permission, except in the case
of brief quotations embodied in critical articles and reviews. For information
contact Permissions, David R. Godine, Publisher, Fifteen Court Square,
Suite 320, Boston, Massachusetts 02108

This edition copyright © 1992 by David R. Godine, Publisher, Inc.

Library of Congress Cataloguing-in-Publication Data
Robinson, W. Heath (William Heath), 1872-1944. The Adventures
of Uncle Lubin / told and illustrated by W. Heath Robinson.
        p.   cm.
Summary: Uncle Lubin attempts to rescue his nephew,
who has been abducted by the horrid Bag-bird.
        ISBN: 978-1-56792-173-1
        [1.Fantasy.] 1.Title.
        PZ7.R5679AD 1992 92-7196
        [Fic] – dc20 CIP AC

Second printing, 2014
Manufactured in the United States of America

DEDICATION

TO E.M.R.

GENTLE INFANT,
For many years I have tried to find some little person to whom I might dedicate this book of wonderful stories; and of all of the small people I met, you, I think, will understand and love my old friend Uncle Lubin.

Yes, for you, dear child, who nearly always try to be perfect and often succeed; you, who are so sorry for those in trouble, and only sometimes cross when you are in trouble yourself; you who hardly ever grizzle, will, I am sure, admire Uncle Lubin, who was always so brave and good.

So, with the hope that you will not object, I respectfully dedicate this book to you; and when you know Uncle Lubin as well as I do, I am sure you will love him.

W.H.R.

CONTENTS

FIRST ADVENTURE

INTRODUCTION

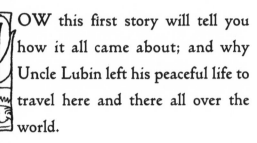

OW this first story will tell you how it all came about; and why Uncle Lubin left his peaceful life to travel here and there all over the world.

You must understand, that Uncle Lubin was a very good man indeed, and that he dearly loved his nephew little Peter, who was nearly always left in his charge.

He used to take him out into the fields and sing old songs to him; he used to gather flowers for him, and dance for him; sometimes he would tell him pretty stories to amuse him.

 UT one hot afternoon while Uncle Lubin was trying to sing little Peter to sleep, he himself fell asleep, quite unmindful of a wicked bag-bird which was watching in the branches overhead.

When the Bag-bird saw that Uncle Lubin was asleep, it stretched out its long neck and snatched little Peter from his arms.

THEN little Peter began to make a great noise, and this woke Uncle Lubin, who saw with horror that his nephew was being carried off in the Bag-bird's beak. He was very frightened, too frightened to move in fact. Therefore he remained where he was. So the Bag-bird got away, and there was nobody to stop it.

HEN Uncle Lubin got onto his feet the Bag-bird was already flying over the next field. "I must follow

it," said Uncle Lubin, and he followed it as fast as he could till evening. Then he saw the Bag-bird fly right up to the moon, and he knew that it would be useless to run after it any more. And he went home, feeling very down-hearted indeed.

SECOND ADVENTURE
THE
AIR-SHIP

ALL the next day the sorrowful Lubin racked his brain to find a way of rescuing little Peter. At last he decided to build an Air-ship, and he set about the work at once.

In a few days the ship was finished, and Uncle Lubin was able to start on his voyage.

Towards midnight he got quite near the moon, and found the wicked Bag-bird perched upon it.

N the other end of it, he quickly

anchored

his

ship

and

climbed

up

the

side,

thinking

all

the

time

that

the

Bag-bird

had

not

seen

him.

OWEVER, just as he was about to catch hold of the bird by the neck it flew off with a loud screech. You will see from the picture that the screech must have been very loud indeed. Only bag-birds can make such screeches. And when Uncle Lubin heard this Bag-bird screeching he felt sure it was laughing at him.

THIS annoyed him very much. All the same he was determined to save little Peter somehow. So he crawled back to his air-ship. But, unfortunately, he found that the end of

the

moon

had

gone

right

through

it

and

spoilt

it

entirely.

19

OW Uncle Lubin was in a great fix. What was he to do? He thought and thought and thought. And at last he said, "I expect I shall have to jump." Holding his hat firmly in his hands to prevent him from falling too quickly, he jumped right off the moon and after a very long drop indeed he landed safely on the earth.

THIRD ADVENTURE

VAMMADOPPER

JUST look at the beautiful boat Uncle
Lubin has built in order that he might
search the seas for little Peter.
In this little boat Peter's
uncle sailed and
sailed for
many
months,
till
he
came
to
an
island
in
the
very
middle
of
the
sea.

ERE he found a little old man
who was crying most bitterly.
"What is the matter
with you?" asked
Uncle Lubin
kindly. The
little
old
man
looked
at
him
through
his
tears
and
told
him
the
following
story:

Y name is Vammadopper, and many
years ago, when I was quite young,
I met a giant who was laughing. I said to him, "Why
do you laugh?" But
he took no notice
of me and
went
on
laughing.
I thought
at first that
he must
be
deaf.

S O I asked him why he kept on laughing again and again. But
the
more
I
shouted
at
him,
the
more
he
laughed,
until
I
could
bear
it
no
longer.

 WAS so angry with him that I drew
my sword to fight him. But when
I rushed at him to make a
stroke he bent down
and with a puff
blew me off
my feet as
though
I
were
a
feather.

VER the clouds he blew me,
and over the mountains and
the seas, till I dropped
on this island
where
I
have
remained
ever since.

35

FOURTH ADVENTURE

THE CANDLE AND THE ICE-BERG

NCLE LUBIN once more set sail in search of little Peter, though not before saying goodbye to poor Vammadopper, and kissing him kindly.

For many months sailed he, till at last he came to the land of Chilblains, where he very quickly became frozen up. Mind you, he wasn't frightened in the least; but soon made up his mind bravely to continue the search on foot.

39

ONE evening, after tramping ever-so-many weary miles over the chilly ice-fields, Uncle Lubin heard the far-away note of the Bag-bird, teasing him and calling him names, from the top of an an iceberg. Lubin ran towards the berg, and as you see in the picture, began to thaw it in two with the flame of his candle.

HE iceberg soon began to totter, and in a little while, it fell. But sad to say it fell on the poor head of Uncle Lubin; while the wicked Bag-bird, with screeches of joy, flew away into the night, still carrying little Peter in its beak.

FIFTH ADVENTURE

THE SEA-SERPENT

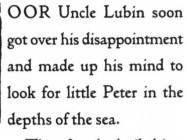

POOR Uncle Lubin soon got over his disappointment and made up his mind to look for little Peter in the depths of the sea.

Therefore he built himself a wonderful boat which could keep under water for a long time and come up again all right.

When he had sailed in this boat many weeks he saw coming towards him a real sea-serpent.

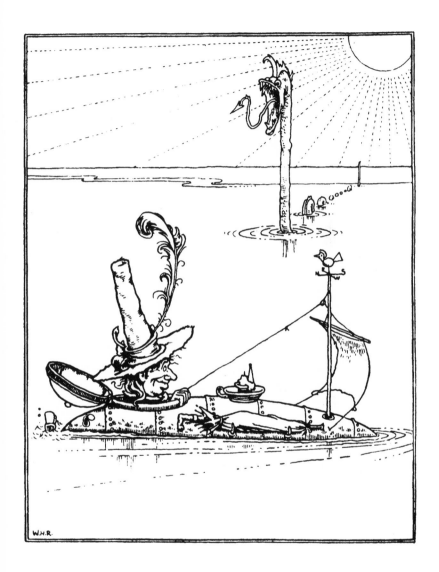

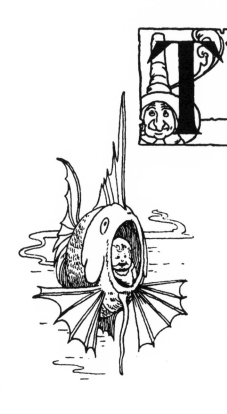

THEN Uncle Lubin at once
allowed his boat to sink,
while the hungry serpent
followed with mouth
wide open,
intending to
gobble him
right
up.

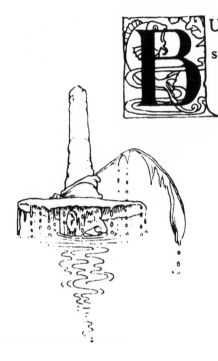

BUT of course the way to kill a sea-serpent is to put some salt on its tail. Uncle Lubin knew this, and when he thought he had been long enough in the water, he raised his boat near the serpent's tail and put a large piece of salt on it.

 NEED not tell you that this
caused the serpent great
pain, so much indeed
that he very
quickly
died,
and Uncle
Lubin
was
able to
go
on his
way
in
search
of
little
Peter.

SIXTH ADVENTURE

THE MER-BOY

ONE day while Uncle Lubin
was still sadly exploring
the depths of the sea,
he came across a
shoal of little
mer-children.
One of the little
mer-boys caught
hold of the side of
Uncle Lubin's ship
and would not let go.
Uncle Lubin tried
to drive him off, but
in vain; so he brought
the little boy to
the surface of
the water.

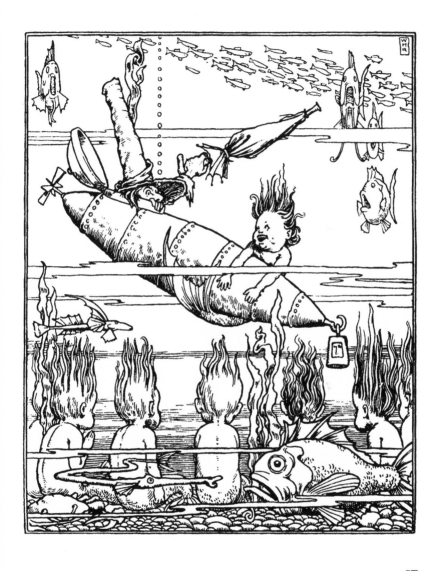

UCH to Uncle Lubin's
surprise he found
that the mer-boy
could talk. He
had many
strange
tales
to tell of his life in the sea, and
among other things he told
Uncle Lubin the following
sad story: "Until quite
lately," he said, "I and
my brothers went to a
school kept by a very
wise old mer-man,
who did his best
to teach us all
we ought to
know."

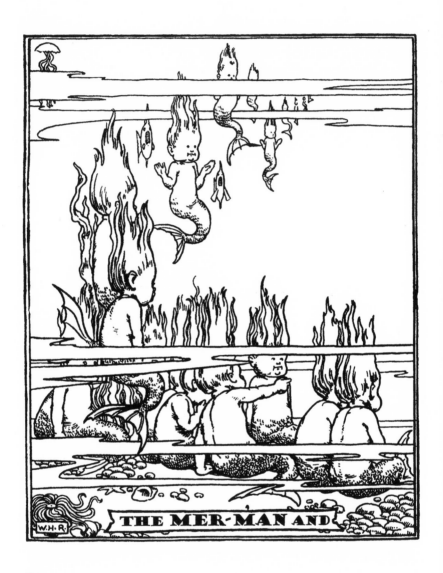

THE MER-MAN AND

THE HUMMING-TOP

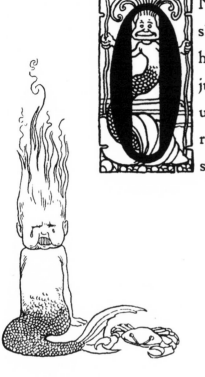

ONE afternoon he had been showing us how to spin a humming-top and he was just beginning to explain to us why it hummed as it went round, when a great fish passing that way with its ugly mouth wide open quietly swallowed the poor old mer-man right up."

"What did you do?" asked Uncle Lubin.

"Well, we did nothing but laugh," said the little mer-boy.

"That was not nice of you," said Uncle Lubin.

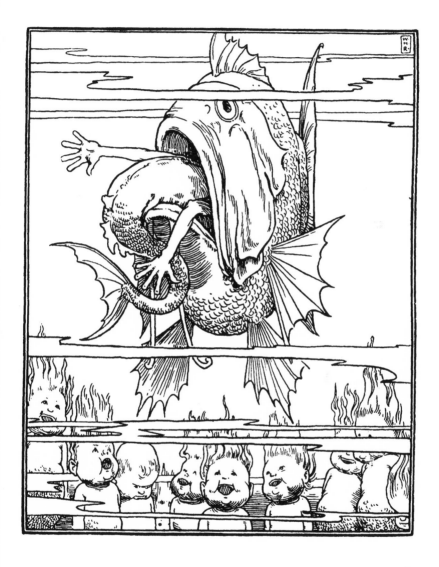

63

SEVENTH ADVENTURE

THE

BOY LUBIN

U NCLE LUBIN was very much obliged to the little mer-boy for telling him such nice stories. And he said to him, "I will now tell you a story. I remember that once when I was a little boy I got lost in a snowstorm. For many hours I wandered up and down trying to find my way home, but all in vain. At last I made up my mind that I had better spend the night in the snow, and I lay down by the side of what appeared to be a hat.

BUT I had scarcely begun to doze off when the hat seemed to jump up of itself, and out of the snow there sprang a funny little old man who looked for all the world like a Jack in the Box.

HIS, of course, alarmed me. And I was more frightened still when the little old man brought out a large sword and said in terrible tones, 'Now I will cut you to pieces.' As I did not want to be cut to pieces, I ran away as fast as my legs could carry me, and without really knowing where I was going. As luck would have it, I ran straight to my home, and was able to sleep in bed that night after all."

EIGHTH ADVENTURE
THE SHOWER

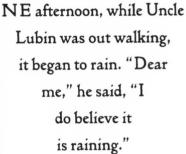NE afternoon, while Uncle
Lubin was out walking,
it began to rain. "Dear
me," he said, "I
do believe it
is raining."
And
he
ran
to
a
shelter,
thinking
the
shower
would
soon
be
over.

 HE rain came down very fast, however. Indeed, Uncle Lubin had never seen it rain so hard before, and he wondered if it was ever going to stop. Soon the whole of the country began to get flooded, and Lubin was

obliged

to

climb

into

the

tree to

prevent

himself

getting

drowned.

HE flood rose higher and higher all after-noon, and at last it nearly covered the top of the tree. "I am going to be drowned after all," said Uncle Lubin. "I rather wish I had not come out to-day."

UT just as he was giving up all hope, he thought of a plan by which he might save his life. He had with him his old umbrella. "I wonder if it would float," he said. He turned it upside down and tried it. The old umbrella floated beautifully. So Uncle Lubin climbed into it and sailed away on his travels.

The Charming

OF THE

Dragon-Snake

ONLY once in the course of his travels did Uncle Lubin become really frightened. In a lonely place and during an awful thunderstorm, he suddenly came across a dragon-snake which, as you will see from the picture, is not by any means a pretty thing to meet. Poor Uncle Lubin shivered in his shoes at the sight of this fearful beast and he felt sure that it would fall upon him and eat him up at once, for besides looking ugly, it appeared to be very hungry.

AFTER a little while, however, Uncle
Lubin's courage returned. He
remembered to have heard
that when you meet a
snake, or for that
matter
a dragon-snake,
the best
thing to
do is to
charm it
with music.
Fortunately Uncle
Lubin had
with him
his old concertina.
On this
he at once
began to play
some beautiful tunes.

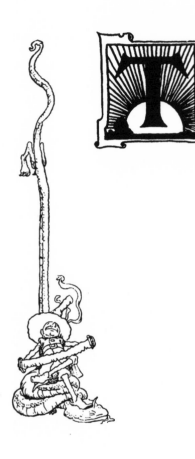

THE dragon-snake was quite pleased with Uncle Lubin's playing and began to dance to it. Indeed the snake danced and danced all night through, and by morning it had danced itself into a tangle, and tied itself into so many knots it died. Playing the concertina all night tired Uncle Lubin very much, but he was glad to have saved his life once again.

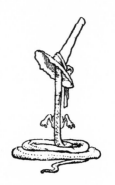

THE DREAM

Y the side of the sea one evening
Uncle Lubin lay down to rest. He
took off his slippers and put his
head on a stone and fell fast asleep.
Soon he began to dream and his
dreams were of little Peter. He
dreamed that the fairies
carried him through
the sky into one
of the most
beautiful
meadows
he
had

ever seen, and there on a beautiful throne with a crown on his
head and the pretty flowers all round him and two wise old
men to take care of him, sat little Peter, who had just been
made King of Fairyland. Uncle Lubin was ready to die with
joy at seeing his little nephew again.

UNCLE LUBIN'S DREAM

OF LITTLE PETER

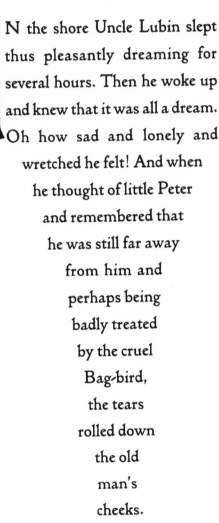

ON the shore Uncle Lubin slept thus pleasantly dreaming for several hours. Then he woke up and knew that it was all a dream. Oh how sad and lonely and wretched he felt! And when he thought of little Peter and remembered that he was still far away from him and perhaps being badly treated by the cruel Bag-bird, the tears rolled down the old man's cheeks.

ELEVENTH ADVENTURE

THE
RAJAH

NE day Uncle Lubin found himself on a curious Eastern tour. The town was full of people, and all of them were crying. "What ever is the matter?" said Uncle Lubin. "Our dear Rajah is in great trouble," replied the people. Uncle Lubin went at once to the palace and found that a wasp had settled on the Rajah's nose, and was biting him as hard as ever it could. And nobody could persuade the wasp to go away.

EAR, dear," said Uncle Lubin, "I
will see to this." So he had the
Rajah taken to the courtyard
and placed upon a mat. Then
he aimed carefully at the
wasp with his gun, and
although the gun burst
in his hands, it
made such
a great
noise
that
the
wasp
was
frightened
and
flew
away.

TWELFTH ADVENTURE

THE FINDING OF LITTLE PETER

FTER all these journeys and adventures Uncle Lubin began to get rather tired, and he almost gave up hope of ever seeing little Peter again. One afternoon, however, he happened to be walking through a grove of palm-trees. In the midst of his walk he was disturbed by a sudden shower of cocoa-nuts which appeared to be thrown at him from the tops of the trees.

HE poor man was really upset by this. But he determined to find out who it was that could be so rude as to throw cocoa-nuts at him, and he therefore set to work to

climb

the

tree

from

which

the

nuts

had

fallen.

111

LL afternoon he climbed,
and all night, and all the
next day. In fact, he did
not reach the top
of the tree until
he had climbed
two nights
and a day.
So
that
the
tree
was
a
very
tall
one.

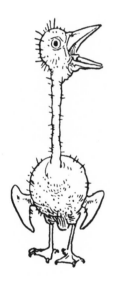

UT when Uncle Lubin did get to the top his heart was filled with great joy. For there, amid the tender young leaves, was the nest of the wicked Bag-bird, and in it, quite warm and cosy and safe and sound among the little bag-chicks, was his dear nephew, little Peter. Of course Uncle Lubin kissed little Peter with all his might, and in a very few moments he had him out of the Bag-bird's nest and was running home with him as hard as ever he could. I am pleased to say that they got home quite safely and lived happily ever after.

A NOTE
FROM THE PUBLISHER

BORN IN LONDON in 1872, William Heath Robinson
came from an astonishing family of artists and illustrators. His
father, Thomas Robinson, was an accomplished wood engraver, and
his two older brothers, Charles and Thomas, were both acclaimed illustrators of children's books, nursery rhymes, and fairy tales. The
times were auspicious for an artist with Robinson's talents; during this
period Edmund Dulac, Walter Crane, Arthur Rackham, William
Morris, Aubrey Beardsley, Kate Greenaway, and Sidney Sime were
all actively lending their talents to book illustration, with extraordi-
nary results. Their influence on Robinson and his work is obvious, as
is the influence of the Japanese master woodcutters whose work was
just then becoming known in the West.

Over the course of his prolific career, W. Heath Robinson illustrated
over sixty titles, but certainly his most famous, and his most enchant-
ing, were the several books he wrote and illustrated himself. These
works contain none of the medieval line of a Morris, accentuated sensi-
bility of a Rackham, or the repressed sexuality of a Beardsley; they are
free, easy, and totally (and innocently) whimsical. Robinson knew
that writing and illustrating books was a two-way street; his work had
to interact with the audience; they had to understand his madcap
inventions. He once wrote, "There must always be this cooperation

between the jester and his audience. It takes two to make a successful joke." Robinson's delightful Uncle Lubin and later Bill the Minder are probably the two best examples of his genius along these lines. He had obvious talents as a great draughtsman, with a quality of sinuous and comic line that only Beardsley could rival, but it was really his daft and bizarre imagination that caught the public's fancy. Here were machines such as never existed; here were adventures that only the master of the comic situation could dream up; here were characters that only a sanguine temperament and equitable disposition could possibly invent.

Robinson's incomparable depictions of impossible machinery described an absurd world in which everything was mechanically plausible. In England, these contraptions gradually came to bear the designer's name (much as Rube Goldberg's did in the United States) and Robinson was thereafter called upon to be everything from a set designer to a muralist. In 1902, shortly after Uncle Lubin was published, Charles Edward Potter, a Toronto businessman, commissioned Robinson to create a series of advertisements in the same spirit. Thereafter, Robinson never lacked for work. Although he proclaimed to the end his complete ignorance of machinery of any kind, he nonetheless went on to invent everything from a six-tier communal cradle for belabored babysitters to a magnetic figure preserver for that roll of fat that often accompanies middle-age. By the 1930s, he was dubbed "The Gadget King" and although he accepted this title with his usual good grace and humor, one gets the feeling he resented it. He thought of himself as an artist and a writer, not a jokester or mechanical prankster. The problem with most humor is that it is never taken seriously (although most of it is very serious) and Robinson's was no exception.

In his autobiography "My Line of Life," he noted that, "My name became so closely associated with humorous work, and a by-word for a certain kind of absurdity, that my signature on more serious drawings was, I admit, disconcerting."

Like all great artists, the core of Robinson's genius was his ability to make us stop and re-examine our world. His incomparable sense of the absurd, of the fantastic, grew not out of a morbid disenchantment with the mundane, or macabre fascination with the outlandish, but rather because he saw so much nonsense in daily life. He celebrated the incongruous, the unlikely, the unexpected. And in this union of the worldly and the otherworldly, the prosaic and the fantastic, he was unique and entertaining. He made the absurd plausible. What's more, he made it attractive. To re-issue this book is to rediscover an original mind at work — one that provokes thought as well as provides great pleasure. We hope all readers will share our enthusiasm.

—DAVID R. GODINE

COLOPHON

THIS EDITION of "The Adventures of Uncle Lubin," closely patterned after the original edition of 1902, was designed and set by Scott-Martin Kosofsky at The Philidor Company in Boston, with assistance from Lucinda Hitchcock. The text typeface is Golden, a reproduction of William Morris's 1892 adaptation of Nicolaus Jenson's Eusebius roman. The display typeface is Goudy Stout, a 1939 drawing that its designer claimed to have created "in a moment of typographical weakness." To our eyes, it has a purity of spirit often missing from Goudy's historically self-conscious designs. This book was printed and bound by Yurchak Printing, Inc., Landisville, Pennslyvania.